Danger by Moonlight

WITHDRAWN FROM
THE LIBRARY

UNIVERSITY OF
WINCHESTER

D1394491

Also by Jamila Gavin

Coram Boy
The Hideaway
The Singing Bowls
The Wormholers
Three Indian Princesses
Three Indian Goddesses

THE SURYA TRILOGY:
The Wheel of Surya
The Eye of the Horse
The Track of the Wind

For Younger Readers
Fine Feathered Friend
Forbidden Memories
Grandpa Chatterji
Grandpa's Indian Summer
I Want to Be an Angel
Kamla and Kate
Someone's Watching, Someone's Waiting

Short Stories
The Magic Orange Tree

JAMILA GAVIN
Winner of the Whitbread Award

Danger by Moonlight

EGMONT

To Isaac

KING ALFRED'S COLLEGE
WINCHESTER

SCHOOL RESOURCES CENTRE

CF/GAV | 0278730X

First published in Great Britain 2002
by Egmont Books Ltd
239 Kensington High Street, London W8 6SA

Text copyright © 2002 Jamila Gavin

Illustrations copyright © 2002 David Dean

The moral rights of the author and cover illustrator have been asserted

ISBN 0 7497 4886 9

10 9 8 7 6 5 4 3 2

A CIP catalogue record for this title is available from the British Library

Typeset by Avon DataSet Ltd, Bidford on Avon, Warwickshire
Printed and bound in Great Britain by Cox & Wyman Ltd, Reading, Berkshire

This paperback is sold subject to the condition that it shall not, by way of
trade or otherwise, be lent, resold, hired out, or otherwise circulated without
the publisher's prior consent in any form of binding or cover other than that
in which it is published and without a similar condition including this condition
being imposed on the subsequent purchaser.

Contents

Chapter 1
False Hope

*I*t is twelve years since my father, Geronimo Veronese, left his family and jewellery workshop here in Venice to seek work at the illustrious court of the Great Mogul, Emperor Shah Jehan in the land of Hindustan.

My father didn't even know that my mother was pregnant with me when he set off. Who knows whether any of the letters she sent with travellers and merchants ever reached him? In the twelve years he has been away, she has only received five messages from him, all sent from the court of Shah Jehan. In the last one he said he was trying again to get an audience with the emperor so that he could beg him to be allowed to go home. Shah Jehan dislikes letting his favourite people go. That was six years ago.

We have a portrait of my father, portrayed as a man of his trade, a jeweller, which my mother assures me is a good likeness. He is painted in his workshop, with all his tools neatly lined up. Displayed on the table is his masterpiece – the painter has caught it well – a jewelled pendant with a diamond of such luminosity that it seems to have been created out of water and moonlight. No wonder it is known as *The Ocean of the Moon*. My brother, Carlo, who has seen the real thing, says it depends on what time of day you look at it. Sometimes, in full summer light, it looks as if it has been made from air and fire, and from rays of the setting sun; at other times, it can seem to be created out of limpid water and moon beams. It is a facet-cut diamond, thirty-five millimetres high and thirty millimetres at its widest point. It is set in a cluster of white jade petals, inlaid with gold, and encircled with pearls, crystals and moonstones, which act as handmaidens to this queen of jewels.

My father had always wanted to go to India. He had heard of the fabulous court of Shah Jehan, and also of the rubies, diamonds, pearls and emeralds which are to be found in Hindustan in great quantity. Mama told us how she had been full of foreboding over the perilous journey he was proposing to undertake. It could take months of travelling with camel trains through wild places and deserts, sailing the seas; always in danger of being attacked by brigands and pirates. 'And who will run the workshop while you are away and provide for us?' she had reasoned.

'Carlo is old enough now – nearly thirteen,' my father had reassured her, 'and have I not trained him well?' Carlo is my eldest brother. 'He has worked by my side since he was six years old and learned well. The lad has an eye for stones and an instinct for design as good as my own, and Giuseppe is learning fast too.' (Giuseppe was my other brother.)

My father was right about Carlo. My father would be proud to see what a fine jeweller he has become, and he has passed many skills on to me. I look up to Carlo as if he was my father, and I do believe he even resembles him – especially now that he has grown a moustache.

It is late. I have been working for hours. Carlo has just told me I can stop as soon as I have completed polishing a set of precious stones.

I stand now on our little balcony overlooking the narrow canal, which enters the Grand Canal just to my left. I stretch my arms above my head flexing my muscles which have become so cramped from bending over my tasks. The sun looks huge enough to set alight the whole of the Grand Canal as it drops into the trembling waters.

Through the shimmering, I see a gondola. It is

coming straight towards me. I blink hard. I can not make out anyone in the brightness but, as the gondolier poles his way into the shadows of the overhanging buildings, I see he carries a single passenger; a strange bundled figure wrapped in some kind of shawl. Then I glimpse something of his head. It too is wrapped in a glittering colourful material such as I have only seen in pictures of the Three Wise Kings of the east. The east! My heart jumps in my chest. 'Carlo!' I cry out, my voice breaking with excitement. Carlo grunts a 'don't disturb me' grunt.

'Carlo! It's Papa! Papa has come home.'

Chapter 2
The Man from Hindustan

I hear the clatter of a stool toppling over as Carlo leaps to his feet and rushes out to join me on the balcony. We look down at the gondola. Its passenger is wrapped so tightly in his shawl, we cannot see his face properly. The gondolier hooks his pole to a mooring and pulls his craft over to the edge. 'Hey! Carlo!' He yells up to our balcony. 'You have a visitor!'

Carlo and I look at each other, our faces transfigured; desperate, unspoken hope brims in our eyes. We rush down the steps into the street. The stranger is paying off the gondolier, then with his shawl flung round his shoulders, he makes to step out of the boat. Carlo stretches forward and takes his arm to help him. The man looks up.

Merciful Mother of Jesus! The expectation in Carlo's face dies in an instant. His disappointment cannot be disguised. I fear our groan of anguish must have seemed offensive and inhospitable. I could not help a cry of bitter reproach, 'You are not our father!'

Carlo recovers himself first. Once the stranger has two feet on the ground, Carlo releases his arm, stands back and bows low apologetically. 'Forgive us, sir! We had a sudden hope that you were our father, returned home from Hindustan at last. Please do not feel disconcerted by our ill manners. Whoever you are, sir, you are most welcome in our home.'

I study our visitor's face and my interest returns sharply. He is of Oriental appearance; a lean, gaunt man, with skin as brown as almonds. His eyes are wide, deep brown with a mocking gaze beneath his sweeping black eyebrows. His long, curved nose reminds me of a bird of prey. His lips are tightened into a thin line, as if afraid of letting out secrets, but now they open into a charming smile as he looks at our bewildered faces.

He loosens his shawl and I glimpse a long barley-coloured linen coat over linen trousers. From a leather belt round his waist hangs a scimitar with a mean-looking edge. His bare sandaled feet are gnarled and hard-skinned from much travel, and I catch sight of a gold ring on one toe.

'Are you from the land of Hindustan?' I ask impetuously.

He tips his head in a strange sideways nod, which seems to be an affirmative.

He turns with outstretched arms to catch his only baggage, a single bundle of sailcloth, which the gondolier tosses him, then at last, he introduces himself.

'My name is Amir Iqbal Khan. I am a Musulman from the land of Hindustan.' He crosses the palms of his hands across his chest and gives a slight bow. 'Am I conversing with the sons of Geronimo Veronese?'

'You are indeed, sir,' replies Carlo. He bows low in return. 'I am his eldest son . . .'

'Yes, Carlo,' the man interrupts knowingly, sizing up the two of us.

'Where is our father?' I burst out again, unable to

contain myself. 'Is he coming home? Is he safe and well? Can you . . .?'

'Hush!' Carlo glares at me to be silent, then turns back to the traveller with an apologetic shrug.

The man waves away the apology and pats my head. 'You must be Giuseppe then?'

I step back sharply, away from his touch.

'Giuseppe is dead,' answered Carlo shortly. 'He died three years ago. We sent a message to my father, but it obviously never arrived. Nor the dozen others we have sent over the years. This is my youngest brother, Filippo.'

Signor Khan clasps his two hands to his heart in a gesture of sorrow, then brushes his right hand first to his lips, then his head, then into the space above his head, as if he sends a heartfelt message of intercession to God himself.

'Please come to our house, Signor Khan. You must be tired from your journey. You will need to bathe, change your clothes, eat and rest. Filippo, run on ahead. Tell Mother to prepare for a guest.'

By the time Carlo and the Musulman arrive at our door, Mother has lit the lamps. Her face flushes at the sight of our visitor removing his sandals at the threshold and bowing low before her. Signor Khan addresses my mother as soon as he is seated, and before he has done more than take a sip or two of his wine. 'Signora! I come with news of your husband, Geronimo Veronese.'

She leans forward with clasped hands. 'Oh tell me, is he alive? Is he well? Have you seen him? Spoken to him? You do not bring me bad news I hope . . .?' Her voice quivers.

'Signora, your husband, to the best of my knowledge, is in reasonable health. I left him near Kabul, in the mountain country of Afghanistan on the north-west frontier of Hindustan. That was eighteen months ago, and he was as well as can be expected in the circumstances.'

'Eighteen months!' we gasped with excitement. A mere eighteen months, when it had been twelve years since my family had set eyes on him.

'He is prisoner of the warlord, Mir Baba, who is known for taking hostages to exchange for money to buy weapons and guns. His price is high, especially for Europeans. It is nearly six years since your father was captured while on his way home from the court of Shah Jehan.'

'So he did get permission to come home,' murmurs my mother.

'I too had been taken hostage,' continues Signor Khan. 'We shared some years together as prisoners. Then, by the grace of Allah, my family raised enough money to release

me. Your father was sure that if someone could go to his home in Venice, his family would find the necessary ransom since, as a jeweller, he had some assets. I said I would go.'

'Why?' We all whisper the question. 'Why would you undertake such a risky mission for the sake of a foreigner?'

'I had made a vow.' Signor Khan's face dipped out of the light of the candle. His voice was light; his sentences rising and falling like short musical phrases. 'Your father fell seriously ill in prison. At the height of his fever, when he thought he was dying, he clasped my hand and made me promise that if I got out, I would find you all. I had made a promise of my own, that if I got out alive, I would make a haj, a pilgrimage, to Mecca to give thanks to Allah for my life. A few months later my ransom was paid and I was freed by the grace of Allah. So, I have been to Mecca and now I am here.'

None of us speaks. Mother twists her hands. Tears fill her eyes. She clears her throat and seems about to speak, when Carlo breaks the silence. 'Mother, I think our guest is tired now. We should preserve Signor Khan from any more questions and let him go to bed.'

Signor Khan is shown where he is to sleep – in Carlo's and my bedchamber. Carlo and I make up mattresses for ourselves in the workshop. One of us always slept there anyway for security. Soon, we have all retired for the night.

We had fallen asleep, curled up under light covers in the far corner, when I suddenly woke up, aware of the door opening and soft candlelight being shielded secretly by a hand. Is it Carlo? No, he sleeps deeply just a few feet away from me. I realise it is the Musulman. What is he doing here? What does he want? He glances round the room. My eyes slam shut and I lie perfectly still, I hear some slight movement and half open my eyes. A light wavers somewhere, and his shadow looms up the wall and halfway across the ceiling. He prowls round the workshop opening cupboards and pulling out drawers in skilled silence. He scrutinises every precious stone and metal, and even the designs of commissions which are stacked in folios on a deep shelf. But he is looking for something in particular, which he doesn't find. At last, I hear the faint creak of the door. He is leaving. I hear a sudden intake of breath. I have to look. I risk raising my head. The Musulman is standing in the threshold, his candle held high. He is staring at something ahead. He sighs, as if in recognition. He pulls the door to and leaves us in darkness.

When I'm sure he has gone back to bed, I creep out of the workshop to stand where he had stood, wondering what had caught his attention.

A trembling splash of moonlight falls on the wall opposite me. My father's pale green eyes glimmer in the portrait. We look at each other. 'Can't you see?' he seems to say. The moonlight strengthens, as if a faint cloud clears from its face. Briefly *The Ocean of the Moon* is spotlit in all its glory.

Chapter 3
The Ransom

The waters of the Grand Canal glitter fiercely in the sun. I shield my eyes as Carlo moves us further and further out across the water. Normally we would have hugged the shade of over-hanging buildings. But there were serious matters to be discussed and Carlo said we must not be overheard.

'What can we do?' I asked feebly. 'How can we . . .? I falter, full of anxiety.

Carlo looked grim. 'The Musulman says we must find at least 3,000 florins. Such money would keep our family for a lifetime. It's impossible . . . except.'

'Except – except . . . Carlo! He knows!' I burst out.

'Knows what?' Carlo looks at me puzzled.

'He knows about *The Ocean of the Moon*. He recognised it in the painting when he came prowling round the house last night. Did father tell him about it? Ask him to bring it? Then why didn't he tell us? Is that what he was looking for in the workshop? If he had found it, I bet he would have stolen it from us and vanished into thin air – the low-down, good-for-nothing . . .'

'Sssh!' Carlo shuts me up. 'I'm trying to think.' He lifts the pole and begins to move on again, as if by exerting himself physically, his brain would also be invigorated and find a solution.

Carlo stops poling. 'We must give it to him.'

'We can't!' I gasp in horror. 'And Father wouldn't want us to – surely!'

'Not even if it means his life?' asks Carlo.

We are silent. He is looking away from me, and I am staring at the reflections in the water.

'But what about him? The Musulman? I don't trust that man!' I burst out fiercely. 'How can we give him any money or jewels, let alone *The Ocean of the Moon?*'

'He knew our names, though, and where to find us,'

murmurs Carlo. 'Only Father could have told him that. But I agree. That doesn't mean we can trust him. He brought no direct message from our father. Who knows how he learned of our existence? That's why one of us must accompany him. One of us must go with him to Afghanistan.'

'With *The Ocean of the Moon*?' I can hardly speak the words.

Carlo nods.

'Will you go with him?' I whisper.

'No, Filippo, you must,' he says firmly.

'Me?' I cry, aghast. 'Me? I've never even been to Verona.'

'You're the only one who can,' says Carlo. 'If I go, how will you keep the business going? You're a good little nipper, but not yet good enough. The rest of the trade will make mincemeat of you. And if I ran into trouble like Papa – and didn't come back for years – what would happen to you and Mother?'

'But what about *The Ocean of the Moon*?' I ask fearfully.

'This?' Carlo puts his hand into his jerkin pocket and pulls out a leather pouch tightened with a drawstring. Casually, he tosses it to me.

I gasp with alarm. Instinctively, my hands fly open and catch it. I clutch the pouch to my chest as though it might leap from my hands into the lagoon. 'Carlo!' I exclaim, shocked by his irresponsible action.

'Look at it,' said Carlo. 'You've never actually seen it, have you?'

I pull open the string and feel inside. My fingers

close over something sharp and cold. I tip it out into the palm of my hand.

A shaft of sunlight strikes the diamond set in the nephrite jade, whose leaves seem as white as lilies. I have never seen so many shades of white – darting with light and reflections – as if the moon and stars are trapped inside the pearls, crystals and moonstones which surround it. I must look ridiculous with my mouth hanging open, for Carlo bursts out laughing. It isn't an altogether pleasant laugh; it is edged with anxiety and fear and all the burden of responsibility that he has been carrying for so long.

'It's . . . beautiful . . . it's fabulous . . .' I can't find the words.

'And, you know what, little brother?' says Carlo. He leans forward, his laughter dying away. 'It's a fake. Papa and I made it together. It was his way of teaching me the trade – and also making an exact replica for security. Even Mother doesn't know. Father only told me where he had hidden the real one.'

'But, Carlo! I can't take a fake. They'll know it. They deal with jewels all the time.'

'The warlord might know or has an expert to hand who has the eye, but our Signor Amir Iqbal Khan, I'll stake my life – he can't tell a good fake from the real thing. You see, I've been testing him. He's not a jeweller, just a small-time trader. He knows a crystal from a moonstone, a garnet from a ruby, but he can't tell paste diamond from the real thing. But – you're right. You can't go with just the fake. So you will take both.'

'We have no choice, do we,' I say quietly, looking him directly in the eyes. 'I'm not afraid, Carlo. I know it's right. If this is the price for our father's life then we must pay it.'

Chapter 4
Terror in the Desert

I sit outside our huge tent beneath a vast black Arabian sky, and hug myself against the cold. It's a question of either choking to death inside the stuffy heat of the tent, with a smoking brazier and the huddle of eight men sitting around sucking on a hookah, which they pass one to the other, or freezing out here in the chill of a desert night.

It is four months already since we left Venice, sailing down the Adriatic on our way to Crete and from there across to Syria.

At first, I was too excited to be homesick. I had hardly been out of Venice in my entire life. I had felt like Marco Polo, when I stood on the harbour and half the neighbourhood turned out to wave goodbye. My mother had showered me with bundles of provisions — dried figs and olives and dates and rice and pickled meats and smoked fish — but she could not hold back the tears flowing down her cheeks in case, like Father, she should never see me again.

It was known that I was going on this journey with a ransom to free our father, but no one knew except Carlo and Mama, that I carried Father's masterpiece. Carlo

28

had dismantled the pendant into separate pieces for safety. Mama stitched the smaller semi-precious stones into my clothes, but *The Ocean of the Moon*, the real diamond, Carlo put in a leather pouch, plaited it into my hair and then stitched it to the base of my scalp – that hurt I can tell you. It was completely hidden by my thick curls and the cap I wore on my head. Even Mama didn't detect it. The fake was in another pouch, which Carlo hung inside my shirt round my neck.

Carlo had been right. A few nights before, Carlo had shown the fake diamond to Signor Khan – just to test him. We sat round the table at home in the dining-room our eyes fixed on him. At first he was silent. He put a magnifying glass to his eye and scrutinised it under the candle flame. After a while, he shook his head in wonder. 'It is a masterpiece.'

Now here I am in the middle of a desert somewhere between Al-Hamad and Basra in a raggle-taggle caravan train of more than a hundred traders and their camels, accompanying a man I am still not sure I can trust — even after four months.

A desert storm the night before last has separated us from the main body of the caravan train, leaving everyone strewn like a broken necklace all along the trail.

For the first time, I'm struck by homesickness, and would give anything to be home. Out here I barely exist. I feel no more significant than one of the grains of sand, which make up this vast desert. I lie back, my body reduced to a speck, and look up at the desolate black sky in which the stars, hard as diamonds seemd to stare down unforgivingly. Oh, Venice! How I long

for your blue lagoons and your streets and bridges; how I long for the sound of the gondolieri singing their songs and the boom of the organ shaking the foundations of St Mark's basilica. Here, five times a day, the Arabs and Signor Khan fall to their knees facing Mecca and call out their prayers, 'Allahu Akbar . . . Ash-hadu-alla-ilaha-illallah!' I wonder which of our Gods is listening.

The chill finally gets to me. I return to the tent to endure the smoke and loud chatter as the traders gamble through the night. No one spares me the slightest glance as I crawl under my rug and finally sleep.

The faintest touch at my neck wakes me. I am paralysed, wondering if I am going to be murdered in my bed. Fingers, lighter than feathers, extricate the fake diamond from the pouch round my neck. I lie rigid, immobile, fearing my throat will be cut if I seem to waken. It must be the Musulman. I knew it. I knew he couldn't be trusted. I want to run away. But that would be suicide. Where could I go? My brain teems with possibilities — but all seem useless. Finally, a restless but compulsive sleep overcomes me. Dreams, homesickness, loneliness and now fear rock me through the night.

I wake. My hand flies to the base of my skull. I feel the lump. The jewel is still there. They'll have to kill me before they can get that, I swear. It is not quite dawn. I go out into the dunes to relieve myself.

The attack comes from nowhere. Here in the desert, a footfall makes no sound. So we didn't hear them coming — the desert bandits. Taking advantage of our party being separated from the rest of the train, they came galloping in on camels, dressed in swirling black robes, wielding scimitars and knives. I run first towards the tents, then away from the tents. Flinging myself over the top of a dune I roll down into a hollow and instinctively dive into the soft sand. The last thing I hear are screams and shouts, before the sand fills up my ears and nose and every nook and cranny of my body. My head is tucked into my arms and I burrow with a desperate life or death energy until I have buried myself. Somewhere, far away, I think I hear my name being called.

It is the rising temperature of the day, which hours later, brings me to my senses. Stiffly, I wriggle out of my grave of sand and slither on my stomach to the top of the dune. I look over. The rising sun is like a vast open mouth that could swallow us all up in one burning gulp. I watch it helplessly. It rises upon desolation and silence. I hear no call to prayer, no shouts of 'Allah Akbar' to welcome the day. I feel abandoned. Lost from the sight of man and God, I stare down on our wrecked and ransacked camp. The bodies of my companions and their camels are scattered everywhere.

I call out softly, 'Signor Khan.'

Silence.

Panic-stricken, I yell, 'Signor Khan!'

I hurtle down the dune and blunder round the remains of the camp. I stumble over bodies; hands and feet, clothes, slippers, weapons and dead camels. I move from one body to the next, looking for him. My hand touches a face. Despite the heat, it is strangely cold. I can't help giving a shriek, and roll away in terror with blood sticky on my fingers.

'Signor Khan!' I howl again and again – though why I call for this treacherous man I do not know.

I hear a snort. A camel. It's alive; kneeling in the sand, still as a sphinx. I had been wary of camels till then. They can be bad-tempered, spit and kick and bite – but this one does not move when I creep up to his rough body and huddle into the shade of its side. I must have slept, relieved to be pressed against another living creature.

The full heat of the day begins to wane. It wakes me. I find the energy to gather together some provisions, a goatskin containing water and a sack of food, which I stow away in saddlebags on the camel. I bundle up two of the warmest rugs I can find and strap them onto his back. I look at the sun. There are about two hours left of daylight. I haul myself up onto the saddle and urge and camel to his feet. To my amazement, he responds to my shouts and digging heels.

I have no idea how to navigate myself across this land, so I put my trust in the camel and God – or Allah. The reins droop between my fingers. I slump back against the camel's hump, with half-shut eyes against the glare of the sun, rocking with a seasick rhythm.

I almost don't see the body of the man spread-eagled face down in the sand.

Chapter 5
Enemies at Court

'Signor Khan! Signor Khan!' It is he. I hate him. He had stolen the jewel and abandoned me. He didn't care about me or my father. Nonetheless, I hold the water bottle to his lips and tip the life-saving liquid down his throat. 'Where's the jewel!' I shake him angrily.

It takes him a long time to recover sufficiently to explain, especially as I was still mistrustful and didn't believe a word he was telling me at first.

'Yes – I took the jewel from round your neck to protect you.' He sighed through his swollen lips. 'The desert bandits came, and they set out to kill all of us. They found your jewel and took it, then left me to die. I called your name, but you didn't answer. I thought you were dead. I just began crawling in the hope that someone would find me.

'You lie,' I weep with fatigue.

'No, No. My plan worked didn't it? I am alive, you are alive, and the jewel is safe.'

'What do you mean?' I gasp. 'You said they took it.'

'Ah yes. They took the jewel in the pouch. They took the fake. But I presume you have the real one somewhere on your body? Huh?' He smiled painfully.

He had known all along.

Now the night is black. The temperature drops like a stone. I shiver uncontrollably. I go to the camel and heave off the rugs. I throw one over the Musulman and the other over me. I am cold, very cold, but still I sleep.

We crossed that desert and arrived, just about alive, at Basra – a hell-hole of a place full of cheats and charlatans. Once again, I was filled with suspicion as Signor Khan unexpectedly decided we should abandon the land route to Afghanistan and pick up a ship bound for Hindustan.

'Why?' I protested. 'My father's in Afghanistan, isn't he?'

'I have contacts at the court of the Great Mogul, the Emperor Shah Jehan and we should get a good price there. Then we can go to Afghanistan and release your father,' he argued.

I suppose it made sense, and I felt a surge of excitement at the thought of going to the court of the

Great Mogul, where my father had been, though I still distrusted the Musulman.

At the harbour, we heard of a Dutch vessel, and soon negotiated space on it. Within the week, we were sailing down the Persian Gulf into the Arabian Sea, heading for Karachi.

They were a jolly crew – and many spoke Italian.
When they heard that our destination was Agra and
the court of Shah Jehan, they told all kinds of stories
about conspiracies among brothers, intrigues,
poisonings and murder. 'Shah Jehan had to kill his
brother and nephews to get to the throne. Now he has
four sons,' an old Dutch sailor told me, 'and you
mark my words, the same thing will happen
with them too.' Then he whispered,
'The Great Mogul has an eye for
jewels. If you have something to
sell for your ransom,' he
tapped his nose as if he
knew I did, 'go to
the emperor first.
Trust no one.'

KABUZ

KARACHI

MOGUL EMPIRE

HINDUSTAN

SEA

* * *

Now it is fifteen days since we left the ship. We are travelling across land, sometimes on horseback, and then within the safety of a camel train. With a shock, I suddenly see the vast walls, towers and shining domes of Agra, the capital city of the Great Mogul. I never dreamed of such magnificence.

While I gaze at the city walls bounding with monkeys, Signor Khan pays off the camel master and hails a sedan chair for us both. We are carried on poles like kings, by four lean, iron-muscled men who run skilfully through narrow twisting streets, avoiding carts

drawn by huge oxen with sharp curving painted horns, the like of which I have never seen, and plunge us through teeming markets, which are more extraordinary even than Venice.

Suddenly, we are beneath the towering walls of the palace fort itself. We go through the first gateway into a vast courtyard, and are set down outside the shaded threshold of the palace of the Grand Vizier whom Signor Khan calls his 'friend'.

It seems to me that we are expected. Uniformed servants greet us with water to drink and to wash our hands and feet. We are shown into a chamber where the Grand Vizier is reclining on silken cushions, being fanned by two servants waving peacocks' tails. After effusive greetings, we are taken to our quarters which have been prepared for us. There, we bathe, and I am given new Hindustan style garments, and am asked to give up my own clothes for washing. Swiftly and without being observed, I extricate the linings of my jacket and breeches, into which the other jewels of *The Ocean of the Moon* are sewn and stuff them into my travel bag. Then I fall back on a bed of silken sheets and sleep for the next thirteen hours.

It is late afternoon the next day when Signor Khan says to me, 'Signor Filippo. Now is the time to show our esteemed and most gracious host *The Ocean of the Moon*, which you have carried so faithfully and bravely about your person.' He eyes up my old clothes which, after washing and drying in the intense Indian sun, I have insisted on wearing again. 'The Grand Vizier will be honoured to cast his perfect eye over the item and decide whether he wishes to purchase it.'

I feel the blood rush to my face. I remember the old Dutch sailor's warning to trust no one. 'I'm sorry, Signor Khan,' I answer in a low firm voice, 'I had hoped to interest the emperor himself in this jewel. Could we not request an audience with him first?'

Signor Khan frowns. He translates my words to the

Grand Vizier. The Vizier looks furious. 'You do not seem to understand,' Signor Khan translates his icy reply. 'Do you think the Great Mogul, who has complete power over millions, will grant you an audience? You – a mere boy, and a foreign boy at that? He is more likely to have you flung into the River Jumuna to be eaten by crocodiles for your insolence.' The Vizier gets to his feet with clenched fists, and I wonder if he is going to hit me.

The two men exchange swift glances. I sense danger. Signor Khan looks at me, his eyes hooded. Is he on my side or not? 'Leave us,' he says. His voice is expressionless. 'The Grand Vizier and I will discuss this further. Go! Explore the gardens.' As I obey, I hear a furious argument break out between the two men.

I wander restlessly into the courtyard and pass through a low arch. I hardly notice the beautiful geometric garden, where waterways bubble between fruit trees and flowering bushes, and marble fountains fling their spray into the sun like scattered diamonds.

A loud commotion draws me to a high brick wall. From the other side come loud voices, the rattle of drums, clashing of cymbals and the high reedy sound of pipes and horns. Filled with curiosity, I scramble up a tree whose branches touch the wall. I swing onto the top of the wall and peer over.

I nearly tumble off with astonishment when I see a massive, decorated beast with ivory tusks encased in gold, swaying into view. Was this . . . could it be – an elephant? Back home, a traveller who had seen most of the world, showed me a drawing of an elephant. Yes, this had a long probing trunk, though heavily painted and decorated, and small beady eyes beneath a wrinkled grey brow, and yes – it had broad leafy ears which flapped rhythmically; but I had no idea any creature on earth was so huge. I find I am eye-level with a howdah, a kind of platform strapped to the elephant's back. Over it is a canopy hung with silken curtains and padded with embroidered cushions on which I glimpse a young boy, no older than six years. He wears glittering clothes, and a colourful jewelled turban is wound round his head. Armed warriors run in front, behind and along side with drawn swords. The people bow respectfully. As the elephant passes by, I want to reach out and touch it.

The boy sees me, points and yells. All eyes stare at me. Fearfully, I turn to drop back down into the garden, when the mahut, the elephant keeper, sitting on top of the animal's head, swings round with his iron hooked club as if to run me through. But the boy yells another command, and instead, the mahut hooks me by my jacket and tugs me off the wall like a troublesome insect. I pitch headlong into the crowd.

Chapter 6

Prisoner of a Prince

My arms are wrenched behind my back. A uniformed bodyguard marches me behind the elephant, through the arched gateway into the emperor's palace itself.

We plunge into the darkness of the interior like

termites burrowing through the walls. We hustle along tunnels and more tunnels, sometimes going up steps, then down, then up again and along — so that I would never have been able to find my way back. From time to time, through arrow slits in the walls, I glimpse the shining River Jumuna far below.

We break out of the intense gloom into light. The wide, sun-bright open air is a shock to the eyes. We are standing on a vast upper terrace with four blindingly gold-capped cupolas at each corner. Peacocks, with vivid blue and green trailing tails, strut and squawk; a leopard snarls on the end of a gold chain; doves fly in

swirling clouds of feathers. Up here, the air is fresher; free from the stench of the narrow city streets. Open doorways lead into cool chambers.

From out of one of these doorways hurtles a small boy, barging into me so hard that I am winded and bent double with pain. It is the boy on the elephant.

He laughs as I gasp for air, and waves away the warrior who has brought me. He comes closer; looking at my boots and fingering the cloth of my shirt. He pushes up my sleeves and examines my arms, and then does the same to my legs, lifting the bottom of my breeches and smoothing his hand across my legs. His nursemaid runs up protectively, but he pushes her away too. It was as if he has never seen anyone quite like me before. He tugs me to my feet and takes my hand. He looks at my fingers and nails and gazes into my eyes — which are the greenish-blue of so many Venetians.

The boy claps his hands and yells an order. After a while, the servant reappears with an old man; he is a shuffling bent old man with a trailing coat and squeaky slippers. The boy points at me and issues a command.

'Portuguese?' The old man asks. I shake my head. 'French? Dutch? English?'

'Italian,' I say.

'Ah!' The old man smiles; perhaps because the Italians hadn't fought battles here in Hindustan, but only came to trade.

The translator tells me I stand before Prince Murad Bakash, the youngest son of the emperor, Shah Jehan. Murad has never seen a white boy before. But though the prince is so young, the old man warns me to show respect; even this young prince can have me beheaded at the click of his fingers. 'I advise you to retreat several steps, lower your eyes, bow your head and cross your hand over your chest,' he says.

The questions begin: what is my name, which country am I from, how long have I been in Hindustan, what am I doing here, am I alone, where is my father?

I am beginning to explain when a harsh voice breaks in. Another boy appears – but older – about my age. He too must be a prince judging by his rich clothes. But his expression is haughty, and he seems keen to demonstrate his higher status. He strides across the rooftop, kicks aside toys and cushions which are scattered around.

A flicker of fear runs across Prince Murad's face. He runs behind one of the ever-present bodyguards, while his nursemaid clasps her hands and bows very low before the older boy.

'Bow. Bow low,' hisses the old translator. 'This is Prince Aurangzeb.'

I obey instantly.

Prince Aurangzeb struts up to me and stands so close I can count the number of diamonds embroidered into his sandals. He flips my chin so that I look up. Our heads almost touch. His eyes are narrowed. He tugs the corner of my of my jacket and knocks my cap to the ground. When I bend to retrieve it, he kicks it out of my reach.

The little boy whimpers, but no one comforts him. No one dares.

'Why are you here?' demands the bully.

Suddenly, I feel defiant. I have been in danger ever since I left Venice. What have I to lose? The thought of saving my father banishes all fear of this boy.

I bow deeply before Prince Aurangzeb and, with my

eyes fixed on his jewelled sandals, I make the speech of my life: 'My name is Filippo Veronese, the son of the jeweller, Geronimo Veronese, who is known to his illustrious majesty, the Great Emperor Shah Jehan, as he was employed by your esteemed father here in the court for six years. That is why I have come here. My father has been taken hostage in Afghanistan. I have brought my father's masterpiece, a pendant he called *The Ocean of the Moon*. We believe it to be beyond price. But we must sell it in order to pay the ransom for my father. Knowing of your illustrious father's passion for precious stones, my family thought it fitting that the Great Mogul Emperor, your father, should be given the first opportunity to see this supreme masterpiece. Perhaps he may desire to purchase it for his own use?'

I had spoken slowly so that the translator could interpret my words. I finish my speech and dare to raise my eyes, though keeping my hands crossed over my chest, and I bow again.

'Show me!' the prince commanded.

'No,' I replied boldly. 'It is for the eyes of the Great Emperor and only his.'

There is a stunned silence. His expression fixes into a slight, cruel smile.

'You will remain here and be our guest,' he says, then with a sweep of his long silk jacket, he leaves.

I had dared to disobey. Again, I feel my fate hangs by a thread. Would Prince Aurangzeb snap his fingers and order my execution?

Chapter 7
The Whispering Walls

I have been here for three weeks now and I do not know if I am a guest or a prisoner. I have a room fit for a prince overlooking the terrace. A narrow gully of fresh water runs past my door and, each evening there is a smell of roses in my bed. Yet I cannot leave and a guard stands outside my door.

Sometimes at night, I hear voices in my room. They seem to be inside the very walls themselves. I wonder about spies, and if secret eyes are watching me. I never even feel for the diamond stitched to the base of my head, in case I give my secret away.

Prince Murad comes to see me almost daily. We rough and tumble, chase each other and play games. The translator comes too. I ask him when I can leave. I am desperate to sell the pendant and rescue my father. But he just shrugs and says, 'You can go when the prince allows it.'

'Which prince? Prince Murad? He likes me. He would let me go, I'm sure of it.'

The old man shrugs and looks cautious, and then I know, I am really a prisoner of Prince Aurangzeb. But why? Does Signor Khan know I'm here?

There are many hours each day, when I'm bored and

I fiddle with things. I wish Carlo could see how everything is encrusted with precious stones. I'm seen rubies and emeralds the size of hens' eggs. He would be amazed. I have examined every object in my room, picked up every vase and ornament, and looked behind every screen and awning.

Fiddling absent-mindedly with the carved knob on an ebony screen, a door opens behind it, in the panelled wall. I can escape. Without waiting to wonder whether I am being watched, I let myself out and begin running down the dark tunnel. I think I have remembered the way I have

gone: first straight, then left up some steep steps, then right and along and up some more steps. I am sure I know how to get back, but when I try I am totally lost.

There is no light. I begin to panic. My whimpers echo in my ears and my breath comes out in gasps.

I hear voices. They seep out of the wall. I press my ear to the cold stone, and I hear as clearly as if I am in the same room as them. Immediately, I recognise Signor Khan and the Grand Vizier. The other is a boy's voice. I recognise its harsh arrogant tones. Prince Aurangzeb!

Though I don't understand their language, I hear my name and *The Ocean of the Moon*. I am transfixed; afraid and unsure which way to go.

I hear more voices. They are on my side of the wall; whispered, urgent, cruel voices. Footsteps advance; I run. I run and run, bumping into the curves of the wall as they twist and turn; stumbling up and down stone steps and on again — but still the voices keep coming.

They are after me. I see an alcove of light. I rush towards it — and nearly plunge thirty feet down, over the edge of a low balcony. Just in time, I clutch the balustrade and fall to my knees. The footsteps race up behind. I cannot move. I feel a hand on my neck; see a glint of metal. A voice screams from below, 'Filippo!'

The hand releases me, and the footsteps flee. Below me is Prince Murad waving frantically. I find myself staring almost blankly down into the most sumptuous chamber I could ever have imagined. Silks and brocades are draped over divans and chairs, rich carpets are strewn across the marble floor and the ceiling is hung with chandeliers of crystal and Venetian glass. The tables and chairs are of ebony and teak, encrusted with jewels, and the pillars and railings look solid gold.

A grand person reclines upon a carved couch — a divan. He is a handsome man with deep-set eyes, a straight narrow nose and a long full beard. Behind him, lavishly uniformed servants fan him with peacocks'

tails, and bejewelled handmaidens sit at his feet. This must be the Great Mogul himself, Shah Jehan.

Two older boys, richly dressed, leap from their divan with hands on swords ready to draw. I realise these must be Prince Murad's two oldest brothers; the eldest,

Prince Dara aged about sixteen and the younger, Prince Sultan Sujah aged fourteen.

There is a commotion of guards and servants, as Prince Aurangzeb rushes in followed by an agitated Grand Vizier, whose slippers flap under his heels as he follows. I try to duck away, but the Grand Vizier has seen me, and there is murder in his eyes.

Everyone is looking up at me. Two bodyguards are suddenly at my side. I am hauled away, my feet dragging and bumping painfully down the passageways and steps. The next minute I am flung face down before the Great Emperor himself.

I feel tears falling from my eyes. I face death, I'm sure of it. I call Carlo, and my mother, I beg my father to forgive me for having failed.

Then I hear Prince Murad's voice. He runs across the room and climbs on to the emperor's lap as only a child can. I raise my head to see him clasp his arms round his father's neck and whisper in his ear. A guard uses his foot to force my head back down.

What a babble of voices. Murad's brothers protest mightily. I hear the Grand Vizier joining in. What are they saying? I can't understand, I can't understand.

Just when I am in my deepest despair, I hear a voice that gives me hope. It is the old translator. They have summoned him.

On a command, a warrior hauls me to my feet, though still forces my head down so that I do not gaze into the emperor's face, but I hear his voice, and it has softened. The guard releases his hold on me, and I stand alone. The old translator comes to me.

'His Esteemed Royal Highness, the Great Emperor, King of the World, hears that you claim to be the son of Geronimo Veronese, who has been captured and held for ransom,' he says slowly.

Oh how good to hear my own native tongue. 'Yes, yes!' I cry, 'and please will you tell His Majesty that I have the most wondrous jewel in the world – *The Ocean of the Moon* — a pendant my father made, which is his masterpiece. No other eyes have seen this except my father and my eldest brother, but I am instructed by my family to offer this wondrous object to His Esteemed Majesty, in all humbleness, and if it so pleases him, to sell it to him so that I can release my father from his prison.'

The old interpreter translates. On the emperor's instruction he says, 'Where is this pendant? His Majesty will look at it.'

I explain that it is broken up into several pieces with the diamond stitched to my scalp under my cap, and that I require a barber to cut it free. Could I be helped in this matter and request space in a workshop to reassemble the piece so that it is worthy enough for the emperor's eyes?

A movement up in one of the high balconies catches my eye. Aurangzeb looks up. I see what he sees. My Musulman. I catch the glance they exchange between them, then I look away quickly. There is something between them, I'm sure of it; something more than a business transaction. I remember the voices I heard on the other side of the wall. Perhaps there is a conspiracy between Signor Khan, the Grand Vizier and Prince Aurangzeb. Didn't the Dutchman warn me about such things?

I am taken to a side room and there await the royal barber. I hope he is not in the pay of Prince Aurangzeb. Nervously, I watch him lay out his instruments. He takes up a very sharp razor and covers my shoulders with a cloth. I bend my head as if for execution.

Two armed guards watch, while skilfully, he shaves away my hair, whistling between his teeth as he does. Until he comes to the pouch, like a large lump, embedded in my hair and fixed to the base of my skull. The whistling stops. His hand pauses – briefly, no one breathes. Then with just a few snips, the pouch comes away with a flood of bleeding. His young apprentice attends to me immediately; mops me up from a bowl of water and binds my head with a clean bandage lined with pungent-smelling herbal leaves.

With the pouch clutched tightly in my hand, the guards escort me out of the palace to the workshop of the Chief Jeweller. All the while, I am guarded by two warriors with hands on swords, but this time, I am grateful.

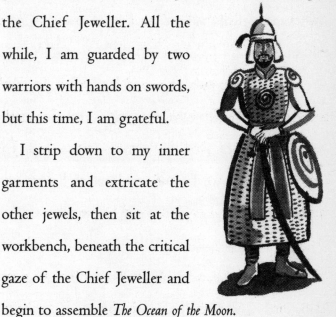

I strip down to my inner garments and extricate the other jewels, then sit at the workbench, beneath the critical gaze of the Chief Jeweller and begin to assemble *The Ocean of the Moon*.

I take the great diamond, over which so much of my blood has poured and, using the tools and glue provided, I fix it into the centre of the nephrite jade setting. Piece by piece I take each pearl, diamond, crystal and moonstone and set them round the queen of all jewels, the fabulous diamond *The Ocean of the Moon*. All the time hearing Carlo's voice in my head instructing me.

At last I stand up. My head swims; everything blurs; I feel faint with the effort, but I have done it! Carlo would be proud. I hold my father's masterpiece in the palm of my hand, touching it, seeing it in reality, for the first time. Was there anything on earth as beautiful as this? My eyes fill with tears. A great rush of homesickness overwhelms me. Suddenly, I don't want to part with it. This is part of my life, my home; it is proof of my father's genius. What if my father is dead already? Giving this up would be like surrendering the family birthright? If only Carlo were here.

I have no time to hesitate as I am marched back again to the emperor's audience hall. To my dismay, the Grand Vizier is still present.

The emperor clicks his fingers. The translator leads

me forwards. With lowered eyes, I approach the Great Mogul and hand him *The Ocean of the Moon*.

The whole chamber falls silent. They stare at it, astonished. He holds it aloft, dangling from its silver chain. Flames and shadows, reflections and shimmering lights enter the stones and make them dance. The diamond flares like the sun, the pearls and moonstones gleam with the purity of angels. The whole cosmos is trapped inside the stones.

'*Subhan Allah! Kya Kehne, la jawab! Yeh toh bilkul kamal ki bath hey.* Unbelievable!' murmurs the emperor with awe. 'Yes, yes!' He shows it off to his sons, still talking enthusiastically.

The translator murmurs to me. 'His Illustrious Majesty is well pleased. He will buy it from you for a good price and declares it will be a perfect gift for his beloved wife when she gives birth to his fourteenth child. Allah be praised.'

The princes gather round admiringly, all except

Prince Aurangzeb. I wonder why. A silent fury distorts his face, and I feel certain that somehow he has been promised it by Signor Khan and the Grand Vizier; that he has some power over them. I wonder if the emperor sees the fury. In any case, he turns to his eldest son, Prince Dara and with a fond embrace, entrusts the precious jewel to him. 'Guard this until the baby is born. Only the queen's beauty compares with the beauty of this creation, and only she must have it.'

He beckons the Grand Vizier to him. They confer with each other. Via the translator, I am told that I will be paid ten thousand gold coins stamped with the emperor's head. Five thousand of these coins will be sealed into a casket which I will take to Afghanistan to gain the release of my father, the other five thousand will be kept here in the charge of the Royal Cashier. My father and I can claim it on our return.

I am to be escorted by an armed guard of twelve men and accompanied all the way by a trusted courtier of the Grand Vizier, Signor Amir Iqbal Khan. As if on cue, there is my Musulman, smiling as he did that first day he arrived in Venice.

Chapter 8

Treachery

We set off in a convoy of three carts, each drawn by four massive horned bullocks and each with a contingent of four armed guards. Alongside too, on horseback, was a further convoy of armed soldiers. I sat in the lead cart with the Musulman. His smile had gone; he looked nervous, yelling at the drivers all the time to get moving, and looking ill at ease. The money for the ransom was in the middle cart, covered with a carpet and surrounded by guards, while the end cart contained our provisions and a further four armed men who were also cooks.

It is four days since we left the court, but it all feels wrong. I hate being without *The Ocean of the Moon*. In my guts I feel sure we shouldn't have sold it; yet in what other way could the ransom have been paid? I still feel embroiled in some kind of conspiracy which I can't fathom, but which I am sure involves Prince Aurangzeb and the Grand Vizier.

I hope the guards are trustworthy. My life depends on them being loyal to the emperor, not his enemies. How easy it would be for them to cut my throat, and escape with the money.

Before we left, Prince Murad had presented me with gifts. One was a silver dagger with a jewel-encrusted handle which I already had sheathed at my waist, and the other was a ruby ring. It fitted my little finger. He cried when I left, and

begged me to return. I was often to see him in my mind's eye, a little prince, all a glitter in his fine clothes, the sun flaring in the sequins and pearls of his wafting silk jacket; his turquoise pyjamas billowing in the hot wind that blew across the river plains.

The lengthy bumping ride by bullock cart from

Agra to Delhi gave me a taste of things to come. There were the appalling tracks we lurched along, full of holes and ruts; the sweltering nights, sleeping in tents, fearful of wild animals and snakes and scorpions, being bitten half to death by mosquitoes. I felt sure that, even if I wasn't eaten by wild beasts, murdered by Signor Khan, or kidnapped by bandits, I would die of fever, for I did get a fever. But Signor Khan insisted we carry on, even though I had a raging temperature and thought I would die. Yet though he attended to me and probably saved my life with his care, Signor Khan was like a man driven by some other purpose, forcing us onwards day by day by day.

From Delhi we travel another fifteen days on the road heading for Lahore, from where we will make the ascent into Kashmir. The Musulman tells me that from there, we will climb up to the Khyber Pass and into Afghanistan. My father is a prisoner in an isolated fort near the boarders of Kafirstan.

We reach the foothills and feel the first chill of the mountains.

One morning, I wake to find the bullocks and the carts gone. I didn't see or hear them go. Signor Khan says the bullock carts could go no further. Only our horsemen remain. We now have mountain ponies, all saddled and bridled, with panniers bulging with provisions.

Although the ponies look small and bony, they are hardy and sure-footed along these narrow mountain tracks, and not

put off by crossing icy streams and terrifying rope
bridges over rushing rivers, which hurtled down from
their snowy sources. I am mounted on a small but wiry
dark brown pony called Sultan. The ransom money is
now strapped in saddlebags to a couple of ponies in
tow with Signor Khan's horse.

It is only when we are trotting single file up a mountain track, that I glance at the rider behind me and realise I don't know him, though I have got to know most of my protectors during our many weeks in each other's company.

When the track broadens sufficiently, I ride on ahead and then, as casually as I can, drop back and back, until eventually I have scanned all their faces. I don't recognise any of them.

'I can't see Asaf Mohammed,' I murmur in an off-hand way pulling alongside Signor Khan. 'And where are the emperor's guards?'

'We've taken on men who know the terrain better than the others. Don't worry about it. Asaf's probably among those who have stayed behind to wait for our return.' He looks me in the eye as he says it, and I look steadfastly back. Once more, I feel in acute danger.

Now I am convinced I will be robbed — probably murdered — but when would it be? Where? Why not now, as we trail along lonely mountain paths, with precipitous drops and furious rivers. What is Signor Khan's plan? I have no choice but to stay with him. Only he knows where my father is being held.

Winter has set in. It has begun to snow. I am thrilled and excited. I have never seen snow before. How strange that I should see it first in Asia and not in Europe. But I soon realise that its beauty is combined with its own stubborn, blinding, blocking, freezing force. We are held up a few days, and Signor Khan rages against our delay. I wonder why. I too am desperate to get on and find my father, yet I can see how there are days when the blizzards sweep across the valleys and that we simply can't move on till the weather changes.

When it does, we move again, halt again and move on again, making small progress day by day. Lofty highlands rise on either side of us, The scenery gets bleaker, browner, but somehow purer. There is a great beauty in the ice-blue skies, the terraced slopes of vines, nuts and fruit trees, and the slender turquoise domes and minarets we begin to glimpse on the distant skyline, as we crossed the pass into Afghanistan.

I have been in Hindustan over three months now, so have at last picked up some Urdu; enough to understand from the talk among the guards that we are avoiding any towns. We bypass the capital, Kabul, and climb high into the surrounding mountains. Our pace quickens. Signor Khan seems nervous. He is short-tempered and shouts at the men to move more quickly. I notice he avoids my eye now and is constantly glancing about him.

One night, rolled up tightly in my buffalo-skin bed beneath the stars, I am unable to sleep because of the cold and because of an unease I cannot shake off. I realise I am not the only one awake. Signor Khan is standing just a foot away from me. He is talking to someone who had arrived on horseback, through I can't hear what they say; can't hear what makes the Musulman give one agonised cry and lean against a rock with his head in his arms. I watch the stranger wheel his horse round and ride away. Signor Khan rocks to and

fro, beating the rock with his fists, howling soundlessly. I watch with terror. I get to my feet. He hears me; turns with the swiftness of a cobra. I see his dagger glinting in his hand. Our eyes meet; his full of tears yet burning with fury and grief. He wants to kill. He could have killed me there and then.

'Why don't you?' I ask.

'Why don't I what?'

'Why don't you kill me?

Signor Khan shakes his head violently, 'Why don't I kill you?'

'You want the money don't you?' I don't flinch and my voice stays steady. 'You wanted *The Ocean of the Moon*. I don't know why you didn't take it in the desert when you could have. Why didn't you?'

He stares through me, then drops his hand and re-sheathes his dagger. The tears hang like icicles on his ravaged cheeks. He glances round him as if afraid we might be overheard, then he drops to his haunches and rests his head between his arms. He waves me to come close. Hesitating and afraid of him, I sit on a rock just a little way off.

For a long time, he says nothing, then he speaks low and fast. 'We are surrounded by spies, so be on your guard. You see, I am as much a hostage as your father.' His whisper is low but harsh. 'The warlord Mir Baba sent me to

collect the ransom, but kept back my own son who he said he would kill if I didn't return within two years. It is one month over the two years agreed.'

I groan with pity. He doesn't pause. 'At first, I admit it, I thought only of getting hold of *The Ocean of the Moon*. Your father told me of it during a fit of fever, when he thought he was dying. He never mentioned it again. I saw it as a way of making my fortune. It was worth far more than Mir Baba wanted for the ransom, but he was in the pay of the Grand Vizier, both of them part of a conspiracy to make Prince Aurangzeb the next emperor, and they needed money. I offered to go to Venice and went to the Mogul court in Agra first to settle a deal with the Grand Vizier.

'The one lie I told you and your family was the amount needed for the ransom. I had to tell you it was thousands so that you would know there was no alternative but to give me *The Ocean of the Moon*.'

'I always knew we couldn't trust you,' I say bitterly.

'I implore your forgiveness.' Signor Khan puts a hand to his heart. 'I know you haven't trusted me. Why should you? As you say, why did I not steal *The Ocean of the Moon*, especially after the attack in the desert? I could have skinned you down to the bone to find it. I knew it must be on your person somewhere. The fake didn't fool me for a moment. But . . .'

'But?' I lean forward; his voice had dropped.

'But, I told you. I went first to Mecca on a haj. I made vows. I am a God-fearing man. I made vows, not only to God, but to your father. I promised to get his ransom. Honour dictated that I keep my vows.'

'But you tried to kill me in the balcony of the Great Hall, didn't you?' I whisper.

'That was not me. The Grand Vizier knew if the emperor saw *The Ocean of the Moon*, he would desire it for himself, and the Vizier wanted it for Prince Aurangzeb. So he tried to have you killed. They are always looking to the future – these kingmakers. The Great Emperor has four sons. Already they are planning twenty years ahead; the whole empire is already dividing itself into factions – especially those who favour Prince Dara and those who favour Aurangzeb. They are filling their coffers with treasure, stocking up their weapons, looking for allegiances among the princely states; even the warlords of Afghanistan are ready to fight to the death for the prince of their choice. There may be four princes, but when the time comes for a new emperor to succeed Shah Jehan, believe me Filippo, only one son will be alive – and he will be the next emperor.'

'So, the Grand Vizier supports Aurangzeb?' I ponder. 'And you? Who do you support?'

Signor Khan's voice quavers slightly. 'If I were a free man, I would support the eldest, Prince Dara. He is a good man with a true heart and a love of the people.'

The words have barely left his lips, and I think he has spoken so quietly that only I could possibly have heard, but there is a swish; a whistle, a drawn breath, a hiss. Signor Khan stays as he is, sitting on his haunches with his head in his hands, but now, a dagger quivers in his back.

Even as he slowly topples over, I grab my goatskin and throw myself sideways. Tumbling, head over heels, bringing with me a small avalanche, I plummet down the hillside into a black void below.

Chapter 9
A Curse

*W*hen I left Hindustan eight months later, I felt I never wanted to see that country again. Forgive me, if I'm emotional. Everything had turned to ashes. It was as though that beautiful masterpiece, *The Ocean of* *the Moon*, was a curse that brought nothing but death and calamity.

Signor Khan was dead, killed by one of Aurangzeb's spies, and his son was dead. That is what the messenger came to tell him that night. How sorry I was now; how racked with guilt as I remembered my harsh attitude to him; how I hadn't asked who the stranger was, nor shown pity for his distress. Only now do I understand the trap the Musulman had been in; why he had been in such a hurry. He had tried to be my friend as much as he could, even though his son's fate hung in the balance. Whenever I was ill, and held up the journey, he looked after me, knowing that it was delaying his return to save his son.

I was found by tribesmen who came upon me at the bottom of a gully half-frozen to death. My guards and the ransom money had melted away, yet the tribesmen seemed to know why I was there; strangers never came that way except those with ransom money. They knew exactly in whose hands my father was and where he was being kept prisoner. We were within a day's walk of Mir Baba's stronghold. They fed me and gave me a blanket, but they looked afraid and keen to be rid of me.

After two days, an older tribesman comes to me and indicates that I should follow him. We walk all day and roll ourselves into yak skins at night. When I awake, the tribesman has gone. Before me are the curving, battle-worn ramparts of the prison fort. I stand before the huge, scarred wooden gates. Can my father be somewhere within those towering walls?

Lounging around outside, smoking cheroots, with spears propped up against the wall are guards; scrawny jagged looking men, with swords at their sides, and I know that they would kill on the slightest whim. They stare casually. I might have been a stray dog, for all the interest they show. Perhaps I no longer look foreign. My skin has become sallow through months in India,

and my body is now quite thin and almost lost in the loose tunic and pyjamas which I wear, having long ago given up my own tattered clothes.

'Chulloh! Get away with you!' One of them shooes me off with his hand. Perhaps he thinks I am a begger.

I speak in slow careful Urdu. 'I am the son of Geronimo Veronese, and I have come to pay his ransom.'

Every head turns. They straighten and take up their spears. One of them disappears through a small door within the huge gate of the fort.

It is a long wait. Why, I haven't the energy to guess. At last, the warrior reappears; his face is blank. He waves me inside. We enter a spacious but bare earthy courtyard, and I am taken across it to a room and thrust inside.

I find myself standing before an older man. His beard is grey and his face puckered with old scars. He lounges on a grubby bolstered mattress smoking a hookah. But I am not deceived by his casualness; by the bowing and deference the warrior showed him, I know this must be a chief.

'So what have I got as payment?' he demands with a betel-red toothed grin, though his eyes do not smile. I hate him. This is Mir Baba, in the pay of the Grand Vizier. I am sure he ordered the killing of Signor Khan and his son, and has already snatched the ransom money from our ponies. He is playing with me, thinking I have nothing.

I put my hand inside my jacket and, from an inside pocket, pull out the ruby and diamond encrusted ring little Murad had given me. I shall have the dagger hidden away. The sarcastic smile vanishes from his face. Greedily, he takes the ring and turns it between his fingers, holding it up in a thin ray of light.

'Please let it be enough,' I pray. I close my eyes and my head goes weak with dizziness. I hear their voices fading as I crumple to the ground.

Someone is shaking me. I open my aching eyes. A strange bedraggled figure stands over me. His hair is long down to his shoulders and quite white, as is his long tangled beard. It is the eyes I recognise, though they seem devoid of sanity. How often had I gazed into those strange greeny-blue eyes of his portrait.

'Father?' I whisper as if waking from a dream.

'Giuseppe?'

'No, Father! My name is Filippo. You don't know me because I was born after you left. We tried to tell you . . .'

He cackles, then weeps. 'Did you bring *The Ocean of the Moon?*'

I get to my feet and sway. He reaches out and, though barely sturdier than I, supports me, then embraces me.

I never answer his question, and he never asks it again. We leave the room. No one challenges us as we stumble out, father and son, our arms linked, and just walk and walked away from his prison.

So it is done. It is sixteen months since I left Venice, but the ransom is paid; my father is free. But for what? They have kept him in a dungeon all those years, till he has become a sick and demented old man, reduced to a wreck in mind and body. Slowly, we leave that hard, pitiless place to begin our long journey home. We reach a trade route through the mountains and by using some of the jewels from Murad's dagger, bargain a place on the caravan train on its way to Lahore and Delhi.

Rambling and mostly incomprehensible, my father questions me about the family, and Venice. He will forget my answers, and question me again and again about home. How badly he wants to see Venice again, but we only get as far as Lahore.

Once more, I feel the curse of *The Ocean of the Moon*. One morning, I wake to find my father dead beside me. He had died quietly, as if like a clock, his body had just wound down and stopped. I bury him according to Muslim rites; there is no other way.

Unable to mourn, I carry on to Agra, my heart utterly devoid of emotion. I would collect the rest of the payment for *The Ocean of the Moon* from the Royal Treasurer, and then return to Venice as speedily as possible.

As I got close to the city, sounds of wailing and lamentation echoed from the balconies and minarets. Then I hear the news: Queen Mumtaz Mahal, the favourite wife of the emperor, for whom he had bought

The Ocean of the Moon, had died in childbirth. The emperor was crazed with grief and the whole kingdom was plunged into mourning.

This wonder, this creation of incomparable beauty, had brought nothing but sorrow and death. How I curse *The Ocean of the Moon;* how I hate this land. All I want to do is get away from this country – this whole continent – as fast as possible.

Thus I leave Hindustan, feeling empty and bereft, never wanting to return.

Chapter 10

The Ocean of the Moon

*I*t is twenty years since these events took place. But now I am back in Hindustan with my brother Carlo, and, though I swore never to return, we are here in the city of Agra. Carlo had always wanted to visit the great

Mogul empire and to pay his respects at our father's resting place in Lahore.

Prince Aurangzeb deposed his father and is the ruler of the empire. On our journey from Venice, we heard of the murders, treachery and many dark deeds which, several years on, eventually led to Prince Aurangzeb taking power. However, he did not kill his father. The Great Emperor, Shah Jehan still lives – they say he is a prisoner in his own palace. Even kings – I think of my father. But my little friend Prince Murad is dead, as are Prince Sultan Sujah and the revered Prince Dara. They fought each other, as my Musulman said they would, and were outwitted and murdered by Aurangzeb and his supporters.

We had thought of bypassing Agra, not wishing to visit such a city of blood, and yet we had also heard that after the death of his beloved Queen Mumtaz, Shah Jehan had built her a tomb, which many fellow travellers told us was of unimaginable beauty, and not to be missed.

So now we stand outside the great arched gateway. It is dawn. Within the high walls, we can see the tops of the trees and clouds of green parrots swooping and screeching as they greet the new day. We hear the call to prayer. The echo reaches us; long, long, reverberations of:

Allahu-Akbar

Ash-hadu-alla-ilaha-illallah

Ash-hadu anna Muhammadar-Rasulullah

Hayya-alassalah

Hayya-alal-Falah

Allahu Akbar

La ilahu illallah

There is a sense of immense peace and goodness. The gatekeepers unroll themselves from their blankets and greet us as we enter the dark green gardens. Night still hangs in shadows and stretches long-fingered across the lawns. The great sky turns silver. Our hearts stop. The light strikes an opaque shape. It is a dome; a vast dome – bigger than any I have ever seen. More and more light pours through a crack in the dawn sky. The dome floats moon-white, like a giant lotus, and lights up the four white minarets standing like handmaidens at each corner.

Carlo hides his eyes as if he has seen a vision. 'Is it really there?' he asks, awestruck.

He looks again. 'Yes, yes! It is still there.'

But I am silent. I remember Shah Jehan holding *The Ocean of the Moon* in his fingers, suspended in the candlelight so that the gems were filled with air, fire, water and ice. I seem to see it again now – but huge and overwhelming, as if we stand within the jewel itself.

I too shut my eyes, expecting that such beauty cannot be real, that it will have vanished when we open them again. But it hasn't. We stare in utter silence, watching the dawn sliding pale pink over the white marble.

We have been standing for three hours. The sun is riding high in an azure sky, the dome is too white, too bright to look at, but still we stand, dazzled, speaking occasionally in hushed voices. Beyond, we see the glittering River Jamuna, and the fields stretching away to a shimmering horizon. A distant camel train picks its way through the shallows. Life goes on.

Only later, as we rode away from that sad beautiful city, did my brother say, 'We have just seen *The Ocean of the Moon*.'

Perhaps that's how it should be. A true masterpiece cannot stay hidden, either in its creator's workshop or in the secret jewel box of a queen. Rather, it is an inspiration for ever and ever. Instead of *The Ocean of the Moon* being a gift for the living, it became, for Shah

Jehan in his grief, transformed into this shining tomb.

Whoever has *The Ocean of the Moon* now, and for whatever dark purpose it has been used, the Taj Mahal, as they call it, will always be a monument to love, and represent all that is good in the world. Perhaps even the life of my father was worth it.

I leave this land in peace.

Postscript

It is known that Geronimo Veronese, the jeweller, came from Venice to Hindustan (India) during the reign of the Great Mogul Shah Jehan, probably to buy precious stones. He could also have been employed by one of the Mogul courts. Contemporary travellers report that he was taken hostage by Afghans. He died and is buried in Lahore.

He is thought by some to have designed the Taj Mahal, built 1632 to 1644.